MINECRAFT
WOODSWORD CHRONICLES

MOJANG

NIGHT OF THE BATS!

Published in the United States by Random House Children's Books, a division of Penguin Random House LLC, 1745 Broadway, New York, NY 10019, and in Canada by Penguin Random House Canada Limited, Toronto. Random House and the colophon are registered trademarks of Penguin Random House LLC.

rhcbooks.com
minecraft.net

Library of Congress Cataloging-in-Publication Data
Names: Eliopulos, Nick, author. | Flowers, Luke, illustrator.
Title: Night of the Bats! / by Nick Eliopulos ; illustrated by Luke Flowers.
Description: New York : Random House, [2019] | Series: Woodsword Chronicles ; book 2
Identifiers: LCCN 2018052179 | ISBN 978-1-9848-5048-5 (hardback) | ISBN 978-1-9848-5049-2 (lib. bdg.) | ISBN 978-1-9848-5050-8 (ebook)
Subjects: | BISAC: JUVENILE FICTION / Media Tie-In. | JUVENILE FICTION / Action & Adventure / General.
Classification: LCC PZ7.E417 Nig 2019 | DDC [Fic]—dc23

Cover jacket design by Diane Choi

Printed in the United States of America

20 19 18 17 16 15 14 13 12

MOJANG
MINECRAFT
WOODSWORD CHRONICLES

NIGHT OF THE BATS!

By Nick Eliopulos
Illustrated by Luke Flowers

Random House 🏠 New York

MORGAN

ASH

HARPER

PO

JODI

MS. MINERVA

DOC CULPEPER

Prologue

IT'S ALWAYS DARKEST DURING THE FLASHBACK BECAUSE THAT'S ALSO WHEN THE ZOMBIES ATTACK!

Six figures stood together in the fading light of day.

Five of them were classmates, friends, and rather short. Some strange recent events had them learning to work together to be a team. But tonight, **the odds they faced seemed overwhelming.**

The sixth figure was taller and wider than the rest. It wasn't human. Its skin was gray and made of iron. Its eyes glowed red.

The friends hoped it could protect them.

"Get ready," said one of them. **"THEY'RE COMING."**

It was true. Not far away, there was a huge group of monsters—zombies and skeletons and hostile mobs. They were only just visible in the glow of the newly risen moon.

And they were heading straight for those six figures.

Chapter 1

BATS, PART ONE: ARE THEY FRIENDS, FOES, OR CLASSMATES?

Ash Kapoor listened carefully for her name. She didn't want to be marked absent by mistake even though her homeroom teacher, Ms. Minerva, had acknowledged the shiny red apple that Ash had placed on her desk upon arriving in class.

Ms. Minerva was trying to take attendance, but there was a **strange sound** coming from the air-conditioning vents. Ash, seated at the back of the room, found it distracting.

"Po Chen," the teacher called.

Ash's friend Po spun around in his wheelchair. He raised his arm like he was lining up a hoop shot. **Po was a master on the basketball**

court. Everyone at school knew him for **his skills as an athlete.** "Here!"

After calling a few more names, Ms. Minerva said, "Harper Houston."

Reading as always, Harper raised her hand without lifting her eyes from her textbook. Ash

thought **Harper was brilliant. She was especially good in math and science.** She also had a great memory. She seemed to remember everything, from algebra formulas to friends' birthdays.

Ash was next alphabetically. She waited for Ms. Minerva to call her name, then raised her hand and made eye contact with the teacher. Ms. Minerva smiled, nodded, and marked Ash down as present.

Ash was new to **Woodsword Middle School.** She'd moved to town only a few weeks ago. But now that she was here, she hoped to get perfect attendance. Ash liked doing her best in all things. It was how she'd obtained so many **Wildling Scout badges.**

From the vents came another small shuffling sound, followed by a metallic clanging. Ash looked around. **No one else seemed to have noticed.**

Maybe the air-conditioning just got loud sometimes.

"Jodi Mercado," the teacher said. Ash smiled. Jodi was the first friend she'd made here. She was creative, fearless, and a little bit weird. **Since Jodi had skipped a grade,** she was younger and smaller than her classmates. She was every bit as smart as the others, though, and Ash thought she was the best artist in the class.

Jodi's big brother was next in the roll call. **He was obsessed with Minecraft,** like Ash herself. It was one of many things they had in common.

"Morgan Mercado," said Ms. Minerva.

"Here!" Morgan said. He spoke loudly. Enthusiastically.

The noise in the vents came back louder. It was almost as if something was reacting to the sound of his voice. There was more shuffling and a small *chirp*.

This time, Jodi noticed it, too.

What was that? she mouthed silently.

Ash gave an **exaggerated shrug,** as if to say *No idea.*

It was at that moment that the door to the classroom flew open, slamming against the wall with a tremendous *bang.*

Their science teacher, Doc Culpepper, stood in the doorway. "Ms. Minerva," she said, out of breath. **"I've come to warn you—"**

Before Doc could finish her sentence, the air-conditioning vent above Ash's head burst open. Dozens of dark shapes flew into the classroom, squeaking and chirping, flapping and fluttering.

"Are those—?" said Jodi.

"Bats!" Ash shouted.

The classroom erupted into chaos. **The kids screamed.** Some ducked low, while others tried to wave the bats away.

Ash hid beneath her desk. She saw that Jodi had done the same.

"This is pandemonium!" said Ash.

"I know!" Jodi replied. "But I kind of love it!"

Ash laughed despite herself. Of course Jodi would see the humor in this.

Ms. Minerva was swatting away bats as **they swooped toward her frizzy hair.** "Everyone, outside!" she instructed. "Please hurry.

But don't run!"

Ash very much wanted to run, but crawling worked well enough. She had to drag her backpack behind her.

Most of the class was already out in the hallway when **Ash had a sudden realization.**

They'd left **Baron Sweetcheeks** behind!

She only hesitated for a moment before turning around and heading deeper into the classroom.

"Ash!" Jodi called. "What are you doing?"

Baron Sweetcheeks was the class hamster. It was Ash's job, as well as Morgan's, to take care of him. **She didn't think the bats would hurt him,** but she also didn't think it was a good idea to leave him behind.

Besides, he hadn't had his morning hamster cookie yet.

Once Ash had crossed the room, she quickly stood up, slung her backpack over her shoulder, and grabbed the hamster's cage. Taking the whole thing would be faster than scooping the hamster out.

But the cage was heavier than it looked.

"**Let me help you,**" said Morgan.

Ash turned to see Morgan had followed her back into the classroom. Then she was almost **smacked in the face by a bat wing.** Okay. Now she was really glad Morgan was there.

With Morgan's help, the cage felt like it hardly weighed anything at all. They ducked their heads low and crossed the classroom in a matter of seconds.

Ms. Minerva **slammed the door shut** behind them.

Ash smiled at Morgan. "Thanks for coming back for me."

He returned the smile. "Thanks for remembering the baron. I was so panicked that I forgot all about him!"

The hamster, for his part, seemed totally unbothered by the whole ordeal. Especially once Ash slipped a cookie into his cage.

"Minerva, I apologize," Doc said. **Full of nervous energy,** she paced the hall while she spoke. "I wanted to warn you about the bats. It didn't occur to me that **my noisy entrance** would set them off."

While Doc never stopped moving, Ms. Minerva always seemed patiently at rest. She put her hands on her hips. "And how did you know the vents were full of bats?" she asked. "Was this another one of your little projects, Doc?"

"I had nothing to do with it!" Doc insisted, waving her hands for emphasis. "I recognized **the sounds** coming from the vents this morning. I've been following the noise from class to class all morning."

Ms. Minerva looked like she didn't wholly believe the science teacher. "At least it's nice outside," she said. "Class, head to the bleachers. I'll be there as soon as I've updated the principal."

"What about Baron Sweetcheeks?" asked Morgan.

"Your hamster can stay with me," said Doc. "It's the least I can do." She snapped her fingers as if remembering something. "In fact, I wanted to speak to

a few of your students anyway, Minerva. May I borrow Ash here, and Harper, Po, and the Mercado siblings?"

Ash and Morgan shared a look. Doc had just named their entire Minecraft team. That couldn't be a coincidence, could it?

Ash wondered if their secret was out. Did Doc know the truth about the game? Or about the message the kids had found while playing it?

There was a high-pitched squeaking sound, and Ash looked over to see a small bat perched over Ms. Minerva's head. The teacher didn't seem to notice.

Ash sighed wearily. Whatever Doc had in mind for them, it couldn't be any more of a disaster than homeroom had been. She hoped.

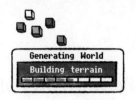

Chapter 2

IT'S ALL FUN AND GAMES UNTIL SOMEONE STEALS YOUR SUPER-SECRET VR PORTAL TECHNOLOGY.

Morgan grinned as he and his friends entered the **computer lab.** *This place,* he thought, *is where the magic happens.*

Maybe literally. He still wasn't clear on the magic-or-super-science thing. All he knew was that Doc had built several pairs of **virtual reality goggles.** The goggles were decorated with strange, glowing symbols that almost looked like words in an **unfamiliar alphabet.** He and his friends had discovered that the goggles allowed them to actually **enter the game Minecraft.** It wasn't like real. It *was* real. And it was so cool!

But his smile fell away when he saw where Doc Culpepper was leading them—straight to the VR goggles hanging from pegs on the wall.

There were five headsets. There were supposed to be six.

"Wasn't there another one of these?" she asked, seemingly talking to herself. "I could have sworn . . . Anyway, there's plenty of room for your hamster here."

Morgan and the others traded a look. After their first few adventures in the game, they had realized that someone had taken that sixth pair. But they didn't know who!

He and Ash slid the hamster cage onto the table.

"Thanks for giving Baron Sweetcheeks a home, Doc," said Harper. Morgan knew that she admired Doc a great deal.

"It's a temporary solution," said Doc. **"We'll have to address this bat problem.** The vents give them access to every room in the school."

Jodi covered her neck. "They're not going to bite us and drink our blood, are they?"

"That's a common misconception," said Doc. "Believe me, those bats are more afraid of us than we are of them. They certainly won't attack you." She tapped her chin. "But still, they're wild animals. They don't belong in a school."

"Aw, they just want an education," joked Po.

"The adults will handle the bats," Doc said. She leaned against a table and crossed her arms, finally standing still. "I asked you here to learn how your after-school project is going. Tell me: **Have you noticed anything strange** as you've been playing Minecraft? Any sign that the goggles aren't working correctly?"

Morgan bit his lip. Where to begin? Whether Doc knew it or not, the goggles went far beyond any sort of virtual reality tech they'd ever seen. **It was amazing**—but it could be scary, too. So far, they'd managed to steer clear of any **hostile mobs,** but Morgan knew that their luck wouldn't last.

And then there was the mysterious message they'd found. **"Beware the Evoker King"** had been written out in huge letters like the famous Hollywood sign. The letters were built out of **obsidian** stolen from one of their own chests during their first big adventure in Minecraft.

Someone else was in the game. And they had no idea who it was. But it *had* to be the culprit who was behind the theft of the sixth headset. So obviously **someone else in their school knew about the goggles' power.**

Morgan simply shrugged. "We have noticed some . . . weird stuff," he said. "But we want to put a full list together for you. We've barely done anything with them yet. You know, we've just been playing Minecraft."

Doc smiled. "Very good. I will look forward to your report. And in the meantime, I'll see what I

can do about **clearing those bats** from your homeroom."

"Thanks, Dr. Culpepper," said Ash. "Let us know if we can help in some way."

"Of course," said the teacher. "Oh, and Ash? Call me Doc, would you? 'Dr. Culpepper' was my father. And my mother. Also one of my grandmothers."

Doc began rummaging through her boxes of electronic equipment. The kids waved farewell, but their teacher's mind was already somewhere else entirely. **Doc was funny like that.** She was somehow super attentive one minute and easily distracted the next.

But Morgan had faith that the bat problem was **as good as solved,** now that Doc was on the case. On their way to the bleachers, he said, "So we're going back to the computer lab after school today, right?"

Po sighed. "I'll be late. I have basketball practice."

"We won't do anything too amazing without you," Jodi promised.

"To be honest, I'm not sure we should do

anything at all," Po said. "Is anyone else worried about the bats?"

"Aw, they're harmless," Morgan said. "Just picture them as Baron Sweetcheeks with wings."

Now that he had said it, he couldn't stop picturing Baron Sweetcheeks with fluffy little wings. And a top hat and a bow tie.

"Uh, Morgan?" said Jodi, bringing her brother back from the world of flying hamsters in formal wear. "Why are you giggling?"

"No reason," said Morgan, **snapping out of his daydream.**

"There's a point I'm trying to make," said Po. "Bats are one of the most common mobs in Minecraft."

"Sure," said Morgan. "We've heard them squeaking when we're down in our mineshaft. But they aren't scary or anything."

"Don't you think it's strange that bats showed up here just after we started playing the game?" Po asked.

Morgan was confused. "You think . . . bats . . . came out of the video game and into our school?"

"It's a statistically improbable coincidence," Harper said. **"And it's weird."**

"But this whole thing is improbable, isn't it?" said Po. "We can go into Minecraft. Who's to say something else can't come out?"

Harper tutted. "That hypothesis completely ignores the law of conservation of mass."

"Now you're just making stuff up," said Po.

"You're the one who's making stuff up!"

While they argued, **Morgan let his mind**

drift. He thought about Po's theory. He didn't think it was very likely that the bats had somehow come to life because of the game. But he had to admit it was possible. And that was a troubling thought.

Bats were one thing. **It was crazy, but what if something else followed them out?** Like a zombie. Or a wither.

Or an Evoker King. Whatever that was, it did *not* sound friendly.

Chapter 3

WHEN ADVENTURE CALLS, ANSWER! ADVENTURE WON'T LEAVE YOU A VOICE MAIL.

After school, Jodi donned her headset and immediately found herself in the game. She **stretched her cube-y arms** and then walked a short distance from the castle she and her friends had built. While they waited for Po

to finish practice and join them, Jodi had time to start on a new sculpture.

It had been about a week since they'd completed the castle. **It was an impressive build,** and Jodi was proud of it. They all were.

But Minecraft wasn't about sitting still. Once the castle was done, they had started new projects. For Jodi, that meant a sculpture park.

So far she'd created an obelisk out of **cobblestone,** an Easter Island–style head out of cobblestone, and a big floating cube . . . out of cobblestone.

Cobblestone and dirt were the two materials they had in large supply. And she was iffy on using the dirt.

Her next project would be a huge staircase that went higher than the castle. But it would be a floating staircase. **There would be no way for a person to get on it.** They would have to admire it from a distance.

She started with a base of dirt, which she would clear away later. She had only just begun placing the cobblestone when Morgan and the others approached. **"I'VE GOT AN IDEA,"** her brother

said. "I think we should go looking for the Evoker King."

Jodi turned her cube head in surprise. "You do?" she asked. "I thought we were supposed to *beware* him."

"'BEWARE' DOESN'T TRADITIONALLY MEAN 'GO LOOK FOR,'" Harper agreed.

"I know what it means," Morgan said. "If he's so dangerous . . . and he's *out there* . . . is waiting for him to find *us* a good idea?"

"But that's why we built the castle," said Harper. "It's meant to protect us."

"The castle can keep mobs out," said Morgan. "I'm worried this EVOKER KING might be something else."

Ash narrowed her eyes. "You think the Evoker King is another player, don't you?"

"It makes sense," Morgan said. "Someone at our school took the sixth headset. They must be using it to enter the game, right?"

Jodi wasn't sure. **"SO YOU THINK THE GOGGLE THIEF, THE OBSIDIAN THIEF, AND THE EVOKER KING ARE ALL THE SAME PERSON?** But why warn us about the Evoker King if they *are* the Evoker King?"

"Maybe to mess with us," Morgan answered. "Or to keep us from wandering into their territory. There's only one way to find out."

"I want to see more of this world, anyway," said Ash.

"AND WE DID PROMISE DOC WE'D GATHER MORE INFORMATION," said Harper. "We can't really do that if we stay in one place."

Jodi looked wistfully at the castle and its sculpture park. **"BUT I ONLY JUST STARTED MY MASTERPIECE,"** she complained, gesturing at the base she'd built for her floating staircase. She added dramatically, "I was going to call it *Don't*

Stair into the Sun."

Ash smiled. "We'll set up camp again eventually," she said. "I'm sure you'll have a chance to build it."

Jodi sighed. "Yeah. The truth is that I could really use some new materials. **I HAVEN'T SEEN ANY SANDSTONE.** And as for wood, it's all oak here. I'd love to find new stuff."

"So it's agreed?" Morgan said.

"We should wait for Po to make it unanimous," said Ash. "But I'm sure he'll be up for an adventure."

Just then, as if summoned, Po came around the corner. **Today he looked like a shepherd.** "Hey, there you are!" he said. "Basketball practice was canceled because Doc herded all the bats into the gym! They're sleeping in the rafters. I got here a few minutes ago and couldn't find anybody."

"Don't get too comfortable,"

Harper said. "We've taken a vote. We all think we should leave the castle to see what else is out there."

"Aw, man," Po said. **"BUT I JUST DYED THE SHEEP!"**

"You dyed the sheep?" said Jodi. She laughed. "This I have to see."

They followed Po back to the fenced enclosure where Beau and Beep lived. Sure enough, one of them was **yellow,** and the other was **blue.**

"I figured now we can finally tell them apart," he explained. "Plus, I'm hoping they'll have a green baby!"

"That is not how science works," said Harper.

"It is here!" Po said happily. **"IT'S JUST ONE MORE REASON I LOVE THIS PLACE."**

"Me too," said Morgan. "And we're not going to let anyone make us afraid of it. Are we?"

They all shook their heads. Po contributed a **"NO WAY!"**

Jodi grinned. "Okay, big brother. You're right. It's time to see what's out there." She held up a wooden sword. "Evoker King, beware *us*!"

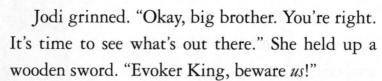

Chapter 4

EVERY JOURNEY STARTS WITH A SINGLE STEP. EVERY STEP STARTS WITH AN ELECTRICAL IMPULSE IN YOUR BRAIN!

Before Harper learned to make things, she had learned to take them apart.

It was the best way to see how things worked, after all. By the time she'd graduated from elementary school, Harper had pulled apart a toaster, a vacuum cleaner, two laptops, and an old TV.

It was done under adult supervision, of course. **Not that her parents knew much about electronics.** Her mother was a painter, and her father was a sculptor. Mr. Houston's specialty was turning trash into objects of beauty. He'd needed circuit boards and TV coils for his projects. So

Harper had been able to help him, while satisfying her own curiosity about gadgets.

Knowing this did not make it any easier to take apart her own work now. But materials were scarce, and she needed redstone dust. The quickest way to get it was to **dismantle the lever mechanism** she'd made for their castle's front door.

"Done," she said, and she held up her newest creation for all to see.

Morgan recognized it at once. "A compass!" he said. "Good idea, Harper."

Jodi, however, was skeptical. "Are you sure we need it?" she asked. "The sun rises in the east and sets in the west here, just like in real life. Couldn't we use that to navigate?"

"Ah, but a **MINECRAFT COMPASS** is special," said Harper. "This will always give us the way to the world spawn point."

"The what now?" said Jodi.

"THE WORLD SPAWN POINT. It's where we appeared on our first day here," Morgan explained. "And since we built our castle quite close to that point . . ."

"We'll always be able to find our way back here," said Harper. "Just in case we want to see your sculptures again. **OR OUR SHEEP!**"

"Yeah, about the sheep . . . ," Morgan began.

"Yes?" Harper prodded.

"Well, I've been wondering . . ."

Jodi asked, "Why are you being so sheepish?"

Then she laughed at her own joke.

Morgan wasn't laughing.

Finally, he blurted, "Do you think maybe we should eat them?"

The girls gasped.

"EAT BEAU?" said Jodi.

"And Beep?" said Harper.

"We're going to need food out there," Morgan said. "That means we're probably going to have to get meat from animals." At the girls' **shocked** looks, he added, "They're not even real! They're just sparkly pixels and a few

41

random bits of computer code."

"MMM . . . SOUNDS DELICIOUS," Jodi said sarcastically. She rubbed her belly for effect.

"Real or not, we're not eating animals that we've named," Harper said.

"Or that I gave to you as a gift!" added Jodi. "Beep represents our sibling bond!"

"Okay, okay," said Morgan. "I'm sorry I brought it up. But we should bake bread before we leave. **AND WE SHOULD GATHER AS MANY APPLES AS POSSIBLE WHILE WE'RE EXPLORING.** We'll need them."

"And we'll need to be smart about who carries what," said Ash. She and Po were walking toward them. "We've just gone through all our chests and discussed what to take . . . and what to leave behind."

"I hate to leave anything behind," said Po. "But we can only carry so much."

"Well, save a slot for this," Harper said. **She held up an iron sword.**

"Ooh," said Po. "That's quite an upgrade."

"I'm making one for everybody," said Harper.

"I hope we don't need them. But I'd rather be prepared."

They headed north, toward the obsidian letters, then turned west toward a range of snowcapped mountains. They decided the mountains would give them a good view. From there, they could decide their next move.

They were moving steadily uphill, which

meant they had to jump frequently. There were no gentle slopes here. **The elevation increased whole blocks at a time.** Soon they were high enough that patches of snow appeared on the ground.

Every time their path took them by a low tree, they would swipe at the leaves. **They were lucky** and found several apples in a matter of minutes.

That wasn't all they found.

"Jodi," whispered Po. He was trembling with excitement. **"JODI, LOOK. LOOK."**

They all looked where Po was pointing. There was an animal in the distance. At first, Harper thought it was a horse. Its neck was too long, though, and its snout too short.

"IT'S A LLAMA!" Jodi squealed. "I want it! I want the llama!"

"Can we keep it?" Po asked.

Not quite sure, Harper turned to Morgan. While she'd logged a lot of hours playing Minecraft, **she'd always been more interested in building** than in taming animals. If there was a way to make the llama a pet, Morgan would know.

"You have to hang on while it tries to buck you off," he said. "It's tricky. And at this elevation, it could be dangerous. **IF YOU FALL . . ."**

Jodi bounded after the llama anyway, jumping rapidly up the steep mountain. "I'll make him love me!" she said. **"YOU'LL SEE!"**

"I want to dye him," said Po, leaping after Jodi. "He should be purple!"

"Don't go too far," Harper warned. The sun had dipped low. Even with iron swords, **she didn't like their odds of surviving a night** in the open.

Ash seemed to read her mind. "We should set up a little shelter," she said. "There's a cave over

there. Let's see how deep it goes."

As always, they were careful to light a torch as soon as they entered the **shadowy cave.** The cave was about a dozen blocks deep. It would be a perfect spot to set up their beds for the night.

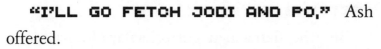

"I'LL GO FETCH JODI AND PO," Ash offered.

"Okay. Harper, watch my back," Morgan said. "I see some coal. I'll gather it for more torches."

"Use this," Harper said. **She handed him an iron pickaxe.** The blocks of coal fell away quickly before the tool. And on the other side . . . **something green glittered.**

"Oh wow," Morgan said. "I don't believe our luck." He used the pickaxe to break apart the green-streaked gray block, and a gleaming green jewel appeared.

"Is that **AN EMERALD**?" Harper asked.

"Yeah. **THEY'RE INSANELY RARE.** It's

definitely worth using an inventory slot to keep it."

"Hey, guys?" Ash said from the mouth of the cave. "You should come see this."

Harper exchanged a look with Morgan. She could tell what he was thinking: *Please don't let Jodi have gotten herself into trouble.*

"I HOPE THE LLAMA DIDN'T START SPITTING AT THEM," he said.

But the llama had gotten away. Jodi and Po stood silent at the peak of the mountain, looking down at something.

"Check it out," Po said.

Harper peered into the valley beyond the mountain.

Situated far below was a small collection of houses. There was farmland, too, and small figures moved about on paths lined with wooden fences.

Harper felt a thrill go through her. "It's a whole village," she said. "WE'RE NOT ALONE OUT HERE."

Chapter 5

BATS, PART TWO: WHAT'S THEIR FAVORITE SUBJECT? AND DO THEY HAVE PLANS FOR THE WEEKEND?

Po couldn't stop thinking about the Minecraft village.

They'd all agreed there wasn't time to explore it before the sun went down. So they'd logged off for the night and returned to their normal lives. Now it was the following day, and classes were moving painfully slowly.

Po wanted to know what surprises awaited them in that village.

There were certainly no surprises on Ms. Minerva's **pop quiz** on *A Midsummer Night's Dream.* When she'd announced it was time for a quiz, the rest of the class groaned—quietly. Although the bats had been confined to the gym and the classroom vents were sealed tight, Ms. Minerva's students still looked at the vents with distrust. **No one wanted to risk setting off another hurricane of bats.**

Po didn't mind the quiz, though. He loved Shakespeare.

He sometimes struggled with reading. His mind was always moving in three directions at once. He had trouble focusing on long passages about how butter was made, or poetic descriptions of sunlight reflecting just so off a tin roof.

But Shakespeare wrote plays. *A Midsummer Night's Dream* was mostly dialogue between characters, plus some speeches called monologues. There were cases of mistaken identity, and **one character was transformed into a donkey.**

Po loved that stuff. He could imagine himself playing any of those roles. He could imagine giving those speeches and feeling what the characters were feeling.

He approached gaming the same way. He didn't just play as himself, as a kid named Po Chen. He imagined himself as a warrior, or a wizard, or a superhero. It's why he was always trying out new skins in Minecraft. **Each one felt like an invitation to be a different person for a little while.**

With basketball canceled until the bats were dealt with, Po wondered if he should try out for the school play. But would the drama kids accept him? Would the rest of the school? Sometimes Po

worried that people only liked him because he was so good at basketball. What if he tried acting and he wasn't any good at it?

"Pencils down, class," Ms. Minerva said softly.

Another small groan rippled through the classroom. Po looked up to be sure, but the air-conditioning vent remained solidly in place.

The bats were still in the gym, then. Po had another day off from basketball practice. Part of him felt guilty about how glad he was.

While the rest of the school was barely putting up with the bats, Doc Culpepper used them as inspiration for a lesson.

"A huge part of a scientist's job is observing," she told the class. "You've all been around these animals. **What have you observed about them?** Ash?"

"Well, they fly. Like birds do. But they have fur instead of feathers. They're obviously mammals."

"That's right," said Doc, rubbing her hands together. "And like other mammals, they give birth to their live young and nurse them with milk. They don't lay eggs the way birds do. What else?"

"They sleep all day," said Jodi.

"Lucky!" Po said.

"Correct," said Doc. "They're nocturnal. In other words, **they're active at night and sleep during the day.** If you were to wait in the school parking lot until dusk, you'd see the whole colony flying away from the gymnasium. They go out at night to hunt bugs to eat. What else? Morgan?"

"They're blind," he said.

"Is that something you've observed?" asked Doc.

"Well, no," Morgan said. "But there's that saying 'Blind as a bat.'"

"Scientists have actually disproven that," explained the teacher. "Bats can see perfectly fine. But **many species do use echolocation to navigate** and to track down their prey. Does anyone know how echolocation works?"

Harper raised her hand. "It's a natural form of sonar," she said. "Bats make sounds, and based on **how the sound echoes** back to them, they're able to perceive details of their environment. Even in complete darkness."

"That's right," said Doc. **"And where do bats live?"**

"At school," Po said, and most of the class laughed.

"Fair answer," said Doc. "But what's their natural habitat? Where are they supposed to live? Do you know, Po?"

Po thought about the bats he'd seen in cartoons. "Caves?" he guessed.

"Some bats do live in caves. But there are no caves in the area. **So where did our bats come from?"**

Morgan raised his hand. "What about the park? I read that some bats live in trees."

"But what are they doing here, then?" asked Po. He'd heard some crazy rumors. Jodi had shared her theory with him that morning. **She suggested that Doc Culpepper herself had**

grown the bats in a hidden basement laboratory. They were all part of Doc's secret cloning experiments . . . until they escaped!

And then there was Po's theory. About how the bats had somehow traveled to their world from Minecraft. Maybe they'd hatched right out of that sixth headset.

Digital bats invading the school was an interesting theory. He wasn't so sure it was the

truth, though. And that led him to his question. "Why would bats relocate to our school and live in our gym instead of staying in their natural habitat?" he asked.

"**That is an excellent question for a young scientist to answer,**" said Doc "I hope you'll all do some research in your spare time. But for now, please clear your desks! It's time for a pop quiz."

The whole class groaned loudly. This time, Po groaned with them.

Doc cackled gleefully to herself. For once, Po thought maybe there was some truth to **Jodi's mad scientist theory** after all.

Chapter 6

VILLAGERS WANT YOUR EMERALDS, NOT YOUR JOKES.

"IS EVERYBODY READY?" asked Jodi. The kids were back in Minecraft, at the top of the mountain. The village was spread out below them.

"Absolutely," said Morgan. "Let's—" He stopped short. "Po, what are you wearing?"

Jodi turned around to look at Po—**and she hopped in surprise!** Ash actually screamed.

"What?" said Po. He was dressed as a clown, with brightly colored hair and a big red nose.

"Why are you dressed like that?" asked Ash.

"I want the villagers to like us. **AND EVERYBODY LOVES CLOWNS."**

"EVERYBODY DOES NOT LOVE CLOWNS,"

said Harper–emphatically.

"I don't know," said Po, rubbing his colorful clown chin in thought. "I think maybe you're wrong this time, Harper."

Jodi giggled. **Avatars couldn't actually roll their eyes,** but she was pretty sure that was what everyone was doing.

"Hey, what do you call a clown on a mountaintop?" asked Po.

Jodi had no idea. "I give up," she said. "What do you call a clown on a mountaintop?"

"Impatient!" Po said. **"LET'S JUST GET DOWN THERE ALREADY."**

Morgan sighed. "All right," he said. "But if the villagers chase you off with torches and pitchforks, *we* are not with you."

"I see," said Po. "And what if they make me their king and shower me with presents?"

"THEN I'LL EAT MY EMERALD," said Morgan.

"Is that really an option?" asked Jodi. "Because I'm sick

of apples. Apples, apples, apples. *Ugh!*"

"Let's go," Ash suggested with a nod of her cube head in the direction of the village. "Maybe they have some real food."

The area was bustling. **Villagers moved about, honking at one another.** If it was a language, it wasn't one Jodi had heard before.

"They don't seem to even realize we're here," she said. She walked up to one in a brown robe. "Knock-knock.

She got no response.

"Oh man," she said. "They don't even go along with knock-knock jokes." She looked over at Po. "I think your outfit is wasted on them."

Po made a sound like a deflating balloon.

"This is mostly what I expected," said Morgan. "They're acting like normal villagers, although they look a bit old-school. Doc clearly isn't running the latest update."

"**MAYBE HER VR TECH DOESN'T WORK WITH NEWER VERSIONS OF THE GAME,**" Harper suggested.

"Or maybe this belongs on our list of weird stuff." Morgan lowered his voice. "Keep an eye out. **IT'S POSSIBLE OUR THIEF IS HERE SOMEWHERE.**"

The brown-clad villager Jodi had approached threw produce toward another villager.

"Uh, is that the sort of thing we're looking for?" she asked.

"Nope," said Morgan. "The ones in brown are farmers. They share food sometimes."

"**GRAB IT!**" said Ash. "We might need that food."

"Hey, check it out," Harper said. She was standing in front of another villager, who was wearing a black robe. "I blinked at this one and **IT OPENED UP A TRADING MENU!**" They had learned on their first adventure that blinking

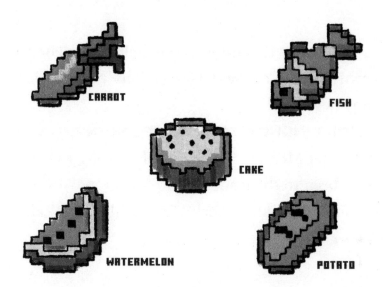

CARROT

FISH

CAKE

WATERMELON

POTATO

their eyes worked like clicking a mouse in the real world. It could open pop-up windows and more. She squinted at some new menu that only she could see. **"THEY'LL TRADE US AN EMERALD FOR COAL.** Do we have extra coal?"

Jodi turned toward Ash. "Are you still keeping track?" she asked.

Ash nodded. "That seems like a good trade to me. **EMERALDS ARE CURRENCY HERE.** We can trade our extra coal for an emerald, then use that emerald to buy something we need."

"Gotcha," said Po. **"EMERALDS FOR BIG RED CLOWN SHOES."**

"You're *not* spending the emerald I just got on clown shoes, Po," said Harper. She held up her shiny new jewel.

"BUT MONEY IS FOR SPENDING." Jodi grinned at Morgan. "You know, it's been *ages* since we've been to the mall."

Morgan grinned back. "All right," he said. "Let's go shopping!"

Jodi lost track of time as she moved from one villager to the next. **It was fun to see what**

each had to offer. They all agreed, however, that no one should actually buy anything without consulting the group first.

Buying food made the most sense. But Jodi had seen farmland on the way into town. **Couldn't they just take food from the fields for free?**

Did it count as stealing if these weren't real people? They were just bits of code, weren't they?

But then, Morgan had said the same thing about the sheep, and Jodi hadn't liked that.

She had just closed her trade window with a purple-robed priest. The priest wanted rotten

flesh, for no good reason Jodi could imagine. **She was about to make a joke about it** when the priest suddenly turned and hurried toward a building.

The villagers were all heading indoors, and quickly. It took Jodi a moment to realize that nightfall had snuck up on them.

"Wow," she said. **"BEDTIME SURE IS EARLY AROUND HERE."**

Harper looked worried. "We should have gone back by now. Our beds are on the other side of the mountain!"

"WE HAVE A LITTLE WHILE BEFORE FULL DARK," said Ash. "If we hurry, we can make it back."

Morgan hesitated a moment. "Okay," he said at last. "But let's go right now."

They passed several buildings, and Jodi could see villagers through the windows.

Then they passed the fields, where **Jodi could see pumpkins and potatoes ready for harvest.** She'd ask about taking food once they were safe.

They were just at the foot of their mountain when **the moon began to rise.**

"We're not going to make it," said Morgan. "I have a bad feeling. . . ."

Then Jodi heard **a distant groan.**

And the rattle of bones.

She looked up.

Atop the very mountain they'd begun to climb, **she could just make out the silhouette of some shambling figure.**

Two shambling figures.

Three.

"Oh no," breathed Ash.

There were dozens of monsters on the mountain.

And they were headed toward town!

Chapter 7

MOBS! MOBS! MOBS! AND THINGS HAD BEEN GOING SO WELL UNTIL NOW . . .

"Back to the houses!" Morgan said. "Quick!"

But the monsters were already closing the distance.

"We'll never make it," said Ash. "We have to fight."

"You're both right," said Harper. She held her iron sword up. "Let's fight our way back to the houses."

They heard a familiar *twang* sound. Morgan knew what that meant. **"THEY'RE SHOOTING ARROWS AT US,"** he said. "Run!"

They ran. Morgan didn't run at top speed, though. He didn't want to lose sight of Jodi. He didn't want to leave *anyone* behind.

So he was the first one to have to fight. A **zombie caught up to him, and he slashed it with his sword.** It flared red, then turned its full attention on him. It reached for

him with rotten hands. It groaned its eerie groan.

But it couldn't touch him. **He knew just how to time his attacks,** and each swing of his sword knocked the monster back. He'd soon defeated it, reducing it to a puff of digital dust and a shred of rotten flesh.

Morgan felt a thrill of triumph, but it didn't last long. In the time it had taken him to defeat one zombie, three more had caught up to him. **He was surrounded.**

"Leave my brother alone!" Jodi shouted. She came up beside him and slashed at one of the zombies. Morgan was impressed. For someone who mostly played in Creative mode, his little sister

was a natural with a sword.

The others were busy with their own fights, but everyone seemed to be holding up. They just might survive this.

"WE'LL GIVE YOU SOMETHING TO MOAN ABOUT," said Harper.

"I'm just glad we can't smell anything here," said Po. "Even with this huge red nose!"

"You came back for me," Morgan said.

"We're in this together," said Ash. **She worked quickly to take out a skeleton**

armed with a bow. She huffed. "So how do we get out of this together?"

"We can do it," Morgan said. "We're winning."

Then he heard a new sound. A low, sibilant *sssss.*

His eyes went wide. "Stop fighting!" he cried. "Everyone get back! Get back now!"

He could just barely see the creeper through the line of zombies. It was flashing white.

He couldn't reach it in time. Couldn't stop it from—**BOOM!**

The creeper exploded. It made Morgan's ears ring. And more than that . . . it *hurt*.

They could actually be hurt here.

"Are you okay?" asked Jodi.

"Yeah," he said. "Yeah, I think so. You?"

"We all got clear in time," Ash said. "Thanks to your warning."

"Our undead friends weren't so lucky," said Harper.

She was right. **The creeper had been good for one thing.** It had totally cleared out the remaining zombies and skeletons. There was a crater in the ground where they'd just been. There was also a lot of random loot left behind—**flesh and bones** and pieces of the landscape.

"We may as well grab this stuff," said Morgan. "You never know—"

Po squeaked in alarm. He pointed off into the distance.

In the light of the moon, Morgan could see **more mobs descending the mountain.**

"This . . . this was just the first wave," Ash said.

"We can make it back to the village," said

Harper. "We have to."

"Okay, let's go," said Morgan. "Hurry!"

They ran down the village's main thoroughfare. All the doors were closed.

"Do we just barge in somewhere?" asked Jodi. Morgan knew what his sister was getting at. **It seemed different to push your way into someone's home when the game felt so real.** Being in the game made the villagers seem a lot more like people. But he'd be a little rude if it helped him and his friends get through the night.

Morgan saw a light in the darkness. One of the villagers had opened the door to their home.

"THAT WAY!" he said.

They all piled in, and Morgan shut the door behind them.

"Will that keep them out?" asked Jodi.

"Yeah," said Morgan. *As long as nothing else explodes,* he thought. "Better to stay away from the doors and windows, though."

It was then that Morgan noticed their surroundings. There were **rows and rows of**

colorful books everywhere he looked.

"We're in a library," he said.

"That's not all," Ash said. "Look."

In the back of the library, there was a gleaming table of obsidian and diamond. A closed book floated above it.

"That's an enchanting table," said Harper with awe. "The things we could make with that . . ."

Morgan took a step closer. The book opened magically at his approach. Strange symbols floated through the air, **as if the book were pulling information from the bookshelves** all around them.

Those symbols looked vaguely familiar to Morgan. He'd seen them elsewhere, and recently. "Wow," he breathed.

Harper edged past him and started flipping through the book. "This would allow us to make better weapons . . . AND POWERFUL ARMOR TO KEEP US SAFE. But we don't have the

materials we need. Not yet."

"One day," said Ash. There was a loud moaning sound from outside. "If we survive the night!"

Morgan peered through the window. **The mobs were moving through the village,** walking down the main path and into the forest on the far side of the houses. There were dozens of them. "I guess we're spending the night in here," he said.

HEH.

Morgan turned toward a white-clad villager, who watched them from across the room. **He knew librarians wore white, but this one looked a little unusual.** She had bright orange hair and a long nose. "You don't mind, do you?" he asked her.

The librarian honked. She threw some food.

"I thought only farmers did that," said Ash.

Morgan sighed. "At this point, I don't know what's a glitch and what isn't. I'VE NEVER SEEN SO MANY ZOMBIES IN ONE PLACE." He double-blinked so he was able to see his inventory . . . and his health. He was missing several hearts. "And I'm injured. So I could use the food."

"EAT UP, BIG BROTHER," said Jodi. Another groan sounded beyond the door. "But no rush. We've got all night."

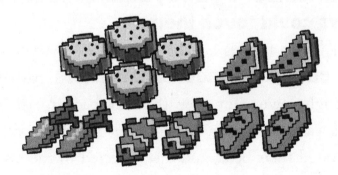

Chapter 8

IT TAKES A VILLAGE TO RAISE A CHILD! IT TAKES A MOB TO RAZE A VILLAGE!

As the sun rose the next morning, no new zombies crested the mountain. The mobs that had entered the village had shambled quickly into the forest, **lumbering away before the sun's rays could touch them.**

The five friends had been stuck indoors while an endless parade of monsters passed through town. But now the way back to their beds was finally clear. They returned to their cave, activated their beds, and disconnected to the real world.

It had been their longest gaming session yet. And Morgan had been hurt! Jodi was actually relieved to hang up her headset and go home for the night. **Homework was going to be a piece of cake compared to fighting zombies.**

The next day at school, the Minecraft team gathered in homeroom before the morning bell rang.

"We have to do something about those pests," Morgan said.

Jodi knew he meant **the hostile mobs that had assaulted the village** and trapped them overnight. But Ms. Minerva overheard him, and she clearly misunderstood which pests he was talking about.

"I know the bats have been disruptive," the teacher said, "but I've been informed that the school board finally has a plan to deal with them."

"I love a clever plan," said Ash. "What is it?"

Ms. Minerva frowned. "Unfortunately, it's not

what I would call a *clever* plan. **They've decided to call in an exterminator.** He'll take care of the problem this weekend."

Jodi gasped. *Exterminator? Take care of the problem?* She knew exactly what Ms. Minerva meant. **"They can't just exterminate the poor things!"** she cried.

"I agree with Jodi," said Harper. **"The bats are acting according to their nature.** They haven't done anything wrong."

"And they're cute," said Po. "They're even cuter than Baron Sweetcheeks."

Now Morgan gasped. "How dare you!" he said. **"Nothing is cuter than Baron Sweetcheeks."**

Po made a kissy face at him.

Ms. Minerva held up a hand for silence. "I'm sympathetic," she said. "I wish there was another solution. But we simply can't continue as things have been." She crossed her arms. "Cute as they may be, they *are* pests."

Jodi bit her tongue. **She'd been called a pest before.** It didn't feel very nice.

And she couldn't help but think there was a better way to deal with this problem.

As soon as they were back in Minecraft, they got to work.

"Grab the beds," Ash said. "We need **OUR RESPAWN POINT** to be closer to the village. Otherwise we'll lose too much time traveling back and forth."

"Why go back at all?" asked Jodi.

"For one thing, I'd like to make use of that enchanting table," said Harper. "It could be a while before we encounter another one. **AND EVEN LONGER BEFORE WE CAN CRAFT OUR OWN.**"

"Maybe we'll get lucky," said Morgan. "Maybe the mobs won't attack tonight."

Jodi could tell by his voice that he didn't believe that was likely.

The mood was tense as they descended the mountain.

"I can make armor and new weapons," said Harper. **"BUT WE'LL NEED MORE IRON."**

"I'm on it," said Ash. "We'll just have to dig and hope we get lucky."

"Don't throw anything out," said Morgan. "If you end up with tons of stone and dirt, we can use that to build walls. With walls, we can force the mobs into a choke point."

"Smart!" said Jodi. **That would make it easier to fight a few mobs at a time.** They wouldn't be overwhelmed and surrounded as quickly as could sometimes happen in the game.

"We should dig trenches, too," said Po. "That'll get us plenty of dirt for walls."

"Good call," said Morgan. "There's not a lot of time. Just do what you can, everyone."

Jodi followed Morgan's gaze to the lowering sun. She felt a thrill of dread run through her. **The dark and the monsters would be here soon.**

Jodi watched anxiously as Harper crafted pieces of armor for them.

"THIS WON'T WIN YOU ANY FASHION AWARDS," Harper said. She handed Jodi an iron helmet. "But you'll be better protected now."

"It's perfect, Harper," said Jodi. "Thanks."

"DON'T MAKE ANY ARMOR FOR ME, Harper," Morgan said.

Jodi snapped her head toward him. "Are you serious?" she asked. "You're the one who got hurt yesterday."

Morgan nodded solemnly. "I know. But there's something I want to try . . . **IF HARPER AGREES** it's a good idea. And it's going to require a lot of iron."

Jodi and Harper watched as Morgan dashed into the nearby pumpkin patch. **He took an axe to one of the pumpkins.**

Harper grinned. "I think I know what you're up to," she said. "Let me help." She put down four blocks of iron in a T-shape.

"I hope this works," said Morgan. He placed the pumpkin on top of the iron.

Their new creation came to life immediately.

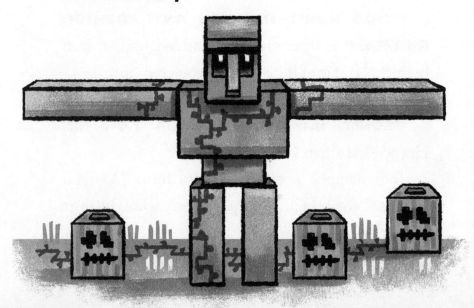

Jodi gasped. "What is that thing?" she asked.

Morgan and Harper had created a tall, intimidating figure. It was iron-gray, with long, powerful arms and soulful red eyes.

"IT'S AN IRON GOLEM," said Morgan. "It'll fight off the hostile mobs. It's on our side!"

"And just in time," Harper said, noting the low sun. "We'd better get into position."

They stood in a row at the foot of the mountain. Although she was an avatar and none of them needed to drink in the game, **Jodi could swear her mouth went dry.**

"Get ready," her brother said. "They're coming."

He was right. The sun had barely set, and already a group of zombies had crested the mountaintop. **There were at least a half dozen of them,** and more appearing every few seconds.

"The golem's up first," said Harper. "Stand back and let it work, people."

As soon as a zombie was in range, the golem

moved forward and attacked. It swung its arms up, **launching the zombie into the air.**

"Ha!" Po said. "Look at 'im fly."

Within moments, the golem had waded fully into the swarm of monsters. Every few seconds, another zombie went flying.

But there were too many. **The golem wouldn't last forever.**

"All right," said Morgan. "Let's show these mobs how we play."

When morning came, Jodi breathed a sigh of relief.

It had been a long and grueling night. **But they had survived it.**

She watched as the last of the mobs disappeared into the trees. Caught in the sunlight, a surviving zombie burst into flame! She chuckled at the sight.

It was hard to feel too triumphant, however. **The village had been thoroughly**

wrecked. Doors had been broken open. Two houses were missing chunks of their walls thanks to creeper explosions. **Arrows were sticking out of every surface.** And the village's crops had been trampled.

"That's right!" Po called after the retreating mobs. "Flee!" **He had dressed like a Viking warrior for the battle.** "My berserker fury is satisfied at last."

"I'm glad you're enjoying yourself," said Morgan. "But I don't know how we can survive another night like that." He held up a wooden pickaxe. **"MY SWORD SHATTERED** midway through the attack. I've been fighting with this thing!"

Harper shook her head. "If only we'd been able to enchant some of our gear. Maybe next time . . ."

"Does there need to be a next time?" asked Jodi. **"MAYBE WE SHOULD JUST MOVE ON."**

"And leave the villagers?" asked Ash.

"Maybe," Jodi said. "I don't know! I wouldn't abandon real people. But they're not real. Are they?"

"They're as real as Beau and Beep," said Ash.

Jodi sighed. "I guess so."

"And anyway," Morgan added, **"I'D LIKE TO GET TO THE BOTTOM OF THIS.**

It's not . . . well . . . It's not normal, is it?" He sighed. "I still don't believe that those bats came from the game. But there is enough **WEIRD STUFF HAPPENING** here that we have to imagine it's possible. We need more information."

"I was just thinking the same thing," said Ash. "Look at what happened to the crops. I know some of the updated beast mobs can trample crops, but I've never seen a zombie mob ruin farmland before."

"Me neither," said Morgan. "But I've *read* about it happening. **IN THE FIRST EDITIONS OF MINECRAFT, ALL MOBS COULD TRAMPLE CROPS."**

Harper looked up. "We noticed the villagers were out-of-date, too. Are we in the original version of the game?"

"No." Morgan shook his head. "Everything else seems up-to-date. I suppose it could be a mod."

"MOD?" asked Jodi.

"It's short for *modification*," explained Ash. **"PROGRAMMERS CAN CHANGE ASPECTS OF THE GAME** with mods. It's not too complicated.

But who would change a detail like that? And why?"

"Or . . . ," said Harper. "Is this the sort of glitch Doc Culpepper warned us about?"

"Hard to say." Morgan shrugged. "Like I said, I want to stick around here and learn more."

"Aye!" cried Po with gusto. **"MY BLADE HUNGERS** for zombie flesh!"

"I'm almost hungry enough to agree," said Jodi. "But I'll settle for apples. Again."

"AND THEN WE NEED MORE IRON," said Harper. **"I HAVE A FEELING WE'LL BE GOING THROUGH MORE SWORDS BEFORE THIS IS OVER."**

Chapter 9

THE GIANT BULLDOZERS IN THE PARK ARE LOVELY THIS TIME OF YEAR.

Ash removed her goggles. They'd been in the game for a whole day and night, but very little real time had passed. Ms. Minerva was in the nearby office. Ash could just make out her curly hair on the other side of the windows. Knowing the teacher, **she was probably absorbed in a book.** Ms. Minerva was a creature of habit.

So were bats. Weren't they? **Ash had been giving the school's strange infestation some thought.**

"There must be a reason the bats are here," she said. "Don't you think?"

Po replaced his pair of goggles on their peg.

"Taco Tuesday?" he suggested.

"I don't think they're here for the cafeteria food," Harper said. "Although you might be onto something. Maybe there are a lot of tasty mosquitoes in the area?"

Ash looked at the clock. **She had an hour before she had to be home for dinner.** "Are you all free for a little longer?" she asked. "I want to do some investigating. Maybe see this park that Morgan mentioned." She tapped her **Supersleuth Scout** badge.

"I'm in," said Jodi. **"But first I need a snack that isn't a digital apple."**

"Tacos!" said Po.

Ash hadn't been to the park yet since moving to town, but she'd heard it was a great place to spend a weekend afternoon. **She was expecting endless fields of grass,** flowers of every color, and a pond where ducklings swam in little rows.

She was not expecting **a giant bulldozer and a crane.** The construction vehicles stood

at the edge of the park, right beside a densely wooded area. **A large section of trees had already been cleared.**

"How long has that been going on?" she asked.

"It must be new," said Morgan. "I was here a few weeks ago. That area was nothing but trees."

"Let's check it out," suggested Harper.

"Can someone push me, though?" asked Po. "This grass is killer to wheel over."

"I gotcha," said Jodi.

They made their way over to the construction vehicles. There was a long chain-link fence blocking off the area. The trees were gone, and the ground was a mess of dirt and broken roots.

"Wow, just look at this section of the park,"

said Morgan. **"They made a real mess."**

"It's a shame," said an old man. He was seated on a park bench with a newspaper in his lap and a sleeping pug at his feet. **"I come here every night to watch the bats, but now they're gone."**

Ash's heart sped up. "Did you say *bats*?"

"That's right." The man nodded. "You wouldn't even know they were here during the day, but they filled the trees. At dusk, they'd all wake up and fly off to find dinner. **Sometimes a hundred of them took flight all at once.** It was a spectacular sight." He sighed.

"I'm sure the condominiums they're building will be just as beautiful. **Not!**" Then he returned to his newspaper.

"So that's what happened," said Harper. She

grew more excited as her mind raced. "That's why the bats are in our school. **Their habitat was destroyed.**"

"We have to stop the construction!" said Jodi. "Maybe if we explained the problem to the construction workers . . . ?"

"It's too late," Po said sadly. "Look at it. The damage has already been done."

"Their home is just . . . gone," said Morgan.

Ash was stricken with sadness at the thought. Not even the sight of a sleeping pug could cheer her up.

Chapter 10

A PROBLEM IS JUST A SOLUTION YOU HAVEN'T FOUND YET.

Fo got to school early the next day. He figured that would be his best opportunity to talk to Ms. Minerva.

He found her in homeroom and told her all about the park and the bulldozed habitat. The explanation was obvious: **the bats had nowhere else to go!**

"That's why they're here," he finished. "It's not the bats' fault. They probably don't even really want to be here. They just needed to find someplace to sleep during the day."

Ms. Minerva smiled at him. But it was a small, sad smile.

"I'm impressed that you and your friends were able to learn all this," she said. "And I'm impressed with your compassion for the bats. But this doesn't really change anything, Po. Regardless of *why* the bats are here, they are here. **And we need them to not be here anymore."**

"But . . . ," Po began. He didn't know what else

to say. He'd already made his argument.

"I'm sorry, Po," said Ms. Minerva. "The exterminator will be here tomorrow. And there's nothing you or I can do to stop him."

"I just can't believe it," Po said later. They were in Minecraft, preparing for another siege. **He had taken the form of a construction worker.** "I refuse to accept there's nothing we can do."

"I know, buddy," said Morgan. "I want to stop the zombies from attacking, too."

"I'm not talking about the zombies," Po said. **"I'M TALKING ABOUT THE BATS!** You know, real life?"

"Oh, uh, sorry," Morgan said. If they could blush in the game, Po thought Morgan probably would blush now.

"I didn't mean to snap at you," Po said. "I'm just frustrated that **LEARNING THE TRUTH ABOUT THE BATS DIDN'T HELP ANYTHING.**"

"Wait a minute," Harper said. She put away her pickaxe and went still.

"Uh, Harper?" said Po. **"IS EVERYTHING ALL RIGHT?"**

"Are you thinking what I'm thinking?" she asked.

"Are you . . . thinking about pizza?" he asked.

She gave him a look.

"Is that a no?" he asked.

Harper shook her head. "No. I'm thinking: **WHAT IF THE BAT PROBLEM AND THE ZOMBIE PROBLEM ARE THE SAME PROBLEM?"**

Ash narrowed her eyes. "What do you mean?"

"Think about it," Harper said. "We keep saying that the monsters are attacking the village. But are they really? **THEY TRAMPLE THE STUFF IN THEIR PATH. THEY FIGHT US WHEN WE STAND IN THEIR WAY.** But otherwise?"

Ash nodded slowly. "Remember the night we hid in the library? They just walked right through town and into the woods on the other side, didn't they?"

"So did the ones who got past us last night," said Jodi. "They ran off into those same woods."

Po's mind reeled at what they were saying. **"YOU THINK THE ZOMBIES AND SKELETONS ARE . . . RELOCATING? LIKE, THEY'RE MOVING FROM ONE HABITAT TO ANOTHER?"** he asked.

"I think maybe they are," said Harper. "They're

relocating from the mountain to the forest. And the village happens to be right in their way."

"Oh man," Morgan said. He hopped in place. "If that's true, then **WE'RE NOT HELPING THE VILLAGE WHEN WE FIGHT THE MOBS.** We're making things worse!"

"But knowing what we know now, we can make it better," said Harper.

"Finally," said Po. **"A PROBLEM WE CAN ACTUALLY SOLVE!** But, uh, how do we do that?"

"We stop fighting the monsters," said Harper, "and we start helping them instead."

SQUEE!

Chapter 11

MOVE ALONG, ZOMBIES—
THERE'S NOTHING TO SEE
HERE!

Just as they'd done the night before, **the kids worked through the daylight hours to prepare for the nighttime siege.** But this time, Harper led them in a different kind of preparation. This time, they had to build.

They started with a bridge—a wide, floating walkway that began at the mountain's peak and went right over the village. They had a lot of "junk" material left over from digging for iron the night before—dirt and several varieties of stone. They used it all now.

Harper decided the bridge should have a high ledge so that falling from it would be less likely. The last thing they needed was for zombies to take the bridge and then fall right off it. **She imagined the chaos of zombies plummeting onto the village like hail.**

An engineer imagined problems like that, then worked to avoid them.

The bridge was a good start. But they couldn't possibly make it large enough to divert every mob.

So they dug a tunnel. It led from the foot of the mountain, under the village, and into the woods beyond. With any luck, most of the mobs that missed the bridge would end up in the tunnel.

Finally, for any strays, they dug a trench around the village. It was deep at the front but became shallow near the rear. **Any mobs that fell into it wouldn't be trapped.** But they wouldn't be able to jump out until they'd bypassed the village.

Even working together, it was a lot to do. They

barely finished before the sun went down.

"IT'S NOT THE PRETTIEST BRIDGE I'VE EVER SEEN," said Po.

"It doesn't need to be pretty," said Harper. "It only has to work." *Please let it work!*

"So what do we do now?" Jodi asked.

"We get out of the way," said Harper. "Our presence could mess everything up. If they see us, THE MOBS MIGHT STILL COME AFTER US."

"Back to the village library, then," said Morgan. "To hope for the best."

"And to talk about our other problem," said Ash. "The real-world one." She grinned. "BECAUSE I THINK HARPER'S SOLUTION HERE MIGHT HELP US SAVE THOSE BATS, TOO."

Chapter 12

BATS, PART THREE: THEY DON'T HAVE TO GO HOME, BUT THEY CAN'T STAY HERE.

"Harper, you're a genius," Ash said as soon as they were back in the real world. "I'm so glad that worked!"

Harper smiled bashfully. "I'm glad, too."

The plan had been a perfect success. Though they waited near the library's window throughout the night, **not a single mob came into view.** The zombies had definitely been out there. Their groans had been audible in the distance. But the zombies steered clear of the village. The crops and houses remained untouched.

"I hope our next plan works just as well as the last one," said Po.

Morgan pointed to the clock. "It's almost dusk. The bats will be leaving the school soon."

"And Ash's Wildling Scout troop is meeting in the gym in half an hour," said Jodi. "Ash, are you sure we're allowed to come with you?"

"I'll explain everything to my troop leader," said Ash. "I'm sure I can convince him to hear us out. But we'll need all the scouts to agree to help us. Otherwise, I don't think we'll get this done in time."

"We'll call our parents and let them know what we're up to," said Morgan. "We should get a teacher's permission, too."

Po pointed to where Ms. Minerva was visible through the window as the teacher stood and stretched. "I know who to ask," he said.

Half an hour later, Ash stood at the head of a crowded table. She rubbed her Awesome Orator badge for luck.

"**Hey, everybody,**" she said. "I'm sorry to take over our meeting like this. Especially because I'm new here. But I could really use some help." She gestured toward Morgan, Jodi, Harper, and Po, who were lined up just behind her. "*We* could use your help," she amended. "**How many of you are students here at Woodsword?**"

A few of the scouts raised their hands. "All right," said Ash. "Well, for those of you who don't go here, let me tell you: It's been an unusual week. **Our school has been totally overrun by bats.** They've been sleeping in the gymnasium's rafters."

Everyone looked up at the ceiling.

"Don't worry. They're not here now. The sun has set, so they're all out hunting. They eat mosquitoes and gnats. They're actually quite helpful!" She rubbed her badge again. "Despite that, they're not exactly welcome in a school. So while they're

away, **I'm hoping you all can find the little cracks and holes** they're using to come and go. If you can fill those holes tonight, they won't be able to get back into the school at dawn."

One of the scouts raised her hand. "But where will the bats go then?" said the girl. "Doesn't that just make them someone else's problem?"

"Good questions," said Ash. She nodded at her friends. **"Just leave that part to us."**

Chapter 13

BATS, PART FOUR:
WE MISS THEM ALREADY.
DON'T FORGET TO WRITE.

Po was at school on Saturday morning. *Saturday!* Not only that, but **he was excited** to be there. If someone had predicted that a few weeks ago, he wouldn't have believed it.

But he wouldn't miss what happened next for anything.

As he rolled up, he could see that his friends were there, too. They were hanging out on the sidewalk when a van pulled up to the front of the school. The vehicle was decorated with images of bats, bugs, and mice. **All the creatures were covered with big red slashes.**

Ms. Minerva came out of the school building.

She saw Po and the others and gave them a big thumbs-up. Then she turned toward **the exterminator** as he shuffled forward. He moved slowly under all his heavy gear.

Ms. Minerva waved him away. "I'm sorry," she said. "It seems we don't need your services after all."

The man was clearly confused. **"Isn't this the school with the bats?"**

"It *was* the school with the bats," answered the teacher. "Now it's the school with students who are intelligent, compassionate problem-solvers." She winked at Po and his friends.

"That's cool," said the exterminator. "How

about roaches? You got any of those?"

Ms. Minerva took him by the elbow and steered him back toward his van. "We can handle things from here," she said. **The exterminator grumbled,** still not sure of what had just happened.

As the exterminator drove off, **Po and his friends exchanged high fives and fist bumps.**

Ms. Minerva approached them. "I had to check the entire school to be sure," she said. "But it's true. There's not a single—"

Suddenly, **Doc came hurtling out the front doors** of the school. "Nobody panic!" she cried. "I can fix our problem! Probably."

"Wow," said Po. "Does *everybody* come to school on Saturdays?"

"I've been here all night, perfecting this," said Doc. **She held up a strange contraption.** It looked like an oversized tuning fork, but it had wires running along it and buttons that lit up like

Christmas lights.

"By using **the principles of echolocation,** my crooning fork should produce a sound that will repel the bats without causing human ears to bleed. Again, *probably.*" She cleared her throat. "I just have to find the things first. **The school is still infested, isn't it?"**

Ms. Minerva smirked. "You missed all the fun, Doc. These five solved the problem for us."

"Follow us," said Ash. "We'll show you how."

The school property went far back. They led their teachers past the main office building. They

led them past the portables. They led them past the playground. And they kept going.

Finally, they came to a wooden structure at the far end of the lawn. **It looked like a shed—** the sort where a groundskeeper would store gardening tools. **But it had dozens of long, thin openings along the top.**

"Has this always been here?" asked Doc.

"No, we built it last night," said Ash. "While my scout troop sealed up the school to keep the bats out, Ms. Minerva helped the five of us put this structure together. We wanted the bats to have someplace nearby to call home."

"We call it the bat house," Po said. "For obvious reasons. Now that I say it out loud, I feel like we could probably do better."

"Oh, thank goodness," said Doc. She shoved her device into her satchel. "Because that piece of technology was completely untested and, if I'm honest, a bit of a long shot."

Ms. Minerva considered the bat house. She ran her fingers over a set of carved initials. "You know, it didn't even occur to me to ask last night," she said. **"Where did you get the materials to do this?"**

Po saw Ash deflate a little. "We had to take apart some of my tree house," she said.

Ms. Minerva smiled sympathetically. "That was very generous of you." Doc nodded in agreement.

"We'll replace it, Ash," Morgan promised. "We'll make it even better than before."

"It's all right," said Ash. **"It was for a good cause.** And Harper gave me some great advice."

Harper nodded. "That's right. Sometimes you have to take something apart to build something even better."

"I think we've all learned a valuable lesson this week," said Po. After a dramatic pause, he added, "And that lesson is . . . not everyone likes clowns."

The kids laughed.

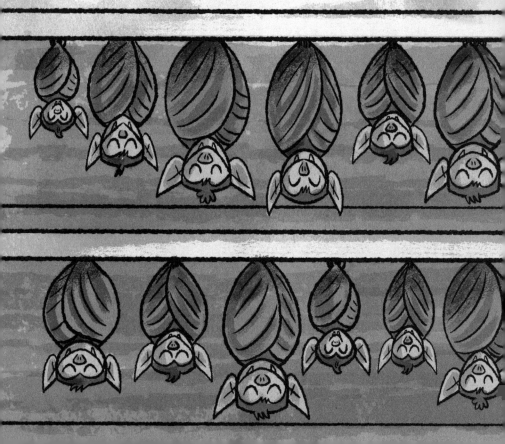

Ms. Minerva shushed them. "They're sleeping," she said, peering in through the bat house window.

"They've got the right idea," said Jodi, rubbing her eyes. "It's been quite a week."

Chapter 14

A NEW DAY DAWNS!
AN UNKNOWN DANGER
LOOMS . . .

A new day dawned on the Minecraft village. Ash and her friends were there to greet it.

But they also had work to do.

They had depleted their inventory while fighting off the monstrous mobs. Their tools and weapons were all damaged. Food was in scarce supply.

Together, they came up with a plan to get themselves back on their feet as quickly as possible.

Morgan focused on digging. **The mountain was rich in mineral ores.** And what they couldn't use, they could trade.

He was careful not to dig too deep, though.

He'd had enough of hostile mobs for a while. At one point, the sound of a single bat squeaking sent him running for the hills.

Jodi was on Overworld duty. She hacked up trees, gathered apples, and tended crops. With the bone meal from defeated skeletons as fertilizer, the crops grew extremely fast.

Po was their runner. **In his custom mail carrier skin,** he would visit Morgan and Jodi, and they would give him any extra materials they didn't need to keep. Then he would deliver those materials to Ash before turning around to do it all over again.

It was Ash's job to trade the extra materials with the villagers. She had been

keeping track of what was in their inventory, so she had a good idea of what they still needed. She was especially excited to trade their rotting zombie flesh to the priest, who then offered lapis lazuli for sale.

Lapis lazuli was a rare ore in a strikingly beautiful shade of blue. No doubt Po or Jodi would love to get their hands on it. But Ash knew of another use for lapis lazuli. She passed it to Harper, who was in charge of crafting new tools to replace their damaged items.

"Do you know what to do with this?" Ash asked as she handed over the lapis.

Harper smiled. "I sure do."

Harper let Ash tag along when she went to the village library. **Together, they approached the enchanting table** with its eerie floating book. As before, the book opened at their approach.

"Magic," Ash breathed. "Real magic!"

"With the lapis, along with all the experience points we got for fighting the mobs, WE CAN DO SOME MAGIC OF OUR OWN." She rubbed her blocky hands together. "So where do we start? A flaming sword? A helmet that deflects arrows?"

Ash thought about it. "But which one of us would wear the helmet? **WHO WOULD GET TO WIELD THE SWORD?** I wonder if there's an option that will benefit all of us at the same time."

"Let's think about it," Harper said. Then she looked around. "Huh. That's weird."

"What is?" asked Ash.

"I haven't seen that librarian at all today," Harper answered. "I assumed she'd be in here."

"That is strange," said Ash. **Villagers were usually very predictable.** She sighed. "One more mystery. Add it to the list."

After a few in-game days of preparation, Ash finally felt confident that they were ready to move on. **"I'M EAGER TO SEE WHAT ELSE IS OUT THERE,"** she said.

"Even if it's not friendly?" asked Morgan.

Jodi hopped in place. "We handled that horde," she said. "We can handle anything!"

"Neither snow nor rain will stop us," said Po, quoting an old postal service motto.

"And I've got something to make the journey a little easier," said Harper. She held up a fishing rod for all to see. **"TA-DA!"**

"Yes!" said Jodi. "Finally, we'll be able to eat something other than apples and bread."

"But it's not just any old fishing rod," Harper said. "I enchanted it, so fishing will be easier."

"OUR FIRST ENCHANTED ITEM," said Po. "Now, that's a special delivery!"

Jodi poked him and said, "Enough with the postal humor. Return to sender, mailman."

"*Male* man?" said Po. "Isn't that redundant?"

Ash noticed Morgan was lost in thought. **"WHAT'S THE MATTER, MORGAN?"** she asked.

Morgan seemed hesitant to say anything. "I've been thinking," he said at last. "We figured out the mobs were relocating like the bats did. But the bats relocated for a reason. They were driven out of their home—out of their habitat."

"I think I see where you're going with this," said Ash.

"Right," said Morgan. "I'm wondering: **WHY WERE THE MONSTERS RELOCATING?** What happened to their habitat? Were they fleeing from something?"

"Fleeing?" said Jodi. "You think the monsters were running away?"

"RUNNING AWAY FROM WHAT?" asked Po.

"Yeah. What could possibly scare a whole horde of zombies and skeletons?" asked Harper.

Morgan turned toward the mountain. **"THE ANSWER'S OUT THERE SOMEWHERE."** He gripped his newly crafted iron sword. **"IT'S UP TO US TO FIND IT."**

MINECRAFT is a game about placing blocks and going on adventures. Build, play, and explore across infinitely generated worlds of mountains, caverns, oceans, jungles, and deserts. Defeat hordes of zombies, bake the cake of your dreams, venture to new dimensions, or build a skyscraper. What you do in Minecraft is up to you.

Nick Eliopulos is a writer who lives in Brooklyn (as many writers do). He likes to spend half his free time reading and the other half gaming. He cowrote the Adventurers Guild series with his best friend and works as a narrative designer for a small video game studio. After all these years, Endermen still give him the creeps.

Luke Flowers is an author-illustrator living in Colorado Springs with his wife and three children. He is grateful to have had the opportunity to illustrate forty-five books since 2014, when he began living his lifelong dream of illustrating children's books. Luke has also written and illustrated a best-selling book series called Moby Shinobi. When he's not illustrating in his creative cave, he enjoys performing puppetry, playing basketball, and going on adventures with his family.

STAY IN THE KNOW!